This
Toby Story
belongs to

AUTUMN

To Gabriel Eng Alvarez, with a hug

LITTLE SIMON
An imprint of Simon & Schuster Children's Publishing Division
1230 Avenue of the Americas, New York, New York 10020
Copyright © 2000 by Cyndy Szekeres
All rights reserved including the right of reproduction in whole or in part in any form.
LITTLE SIMON and colophon are registered trademarks of Simon & Schuster.
Manufactured in China
First Edition
2 4 6 8 10 9 7 5 3 1
ISBN 0-689-82651-6
Library of Congress Control Number 00-133121

Toby's New Brother

by Cyndy Szekeres

LITTLE SIMON

New York   London   Toronto   Sydney   Singapore

Wrapped in a soft, woolly blanket,
in a cradle that once held Toby,
is his brand-new baby brother.

Toby looks at him.
"He's awfully small."

Mama puts the baby on Toby's lap.
He counts the baby's toes and strokes his
furry head. "What little, bitty paws he has."

Toby smiles at his brother.
The baby curls a tiny paw
around Toby's finger.

Toby giggles and the baby smiles.
Then curdly milk dribbles from his
mouth—all over Toby!

Toby needs clean clothes. Since it is almost bedtime, Toby puts on his pajamas.

He is ready to hear his favorite story.

Mama gives Toby the storybook.
"I'll be with you in a minute," she tells
him with a kiss.

"The baby needs to be cleaned
and changed."

"Babies are stinky and noisy," Toby complains.
"Most of the time they smell sweet and they
gurgle and coo," Daddy assures him.

"Can we send him back now?" Toby asks.
"No, my precious mouse. Someday you'll
be very best friends," his mama says.

Toby's head droops lower . . . and lower.

"I need a hug," he whimpers.

Daddy cuddles Toby on his lap. "Mama is taking care of the baby, because he is too little. He can't take care of himself."

"Do you know what other things your brother can't do yet?" he asks Toby.

"He can't share any cookies with Daddy."

"He can't put puzzles together with Mama."

"He doesn't have any words yet, but do you know what he does have?" Daddy laughs. "He has the very best, most important someone—a BIG BROTHER!"

"Big brothers play ball with their mama."

"Big brothers build things with their daddy."

"And they get lots of big brother kisses."
Mama, Daddy, and Toby hug and kiss.
Hercules joins them too.

-2003-

Love,

Grama

(Diane)